GAME ON!

BREAK
TO THE GOAL

BY BRANDON TERRELL

STORY
LIBRARY

www.12StoryLibrary.com

12-Story Library is an imprint of Peterson Publishing Company and Press Room Editions.

Produced for 12-Story Library by Red Line Editorial

Photographs ©: Shutterstock Images, cover

Cover Design: Emily Love

ISBN
978-1-63235-045-9 (hardcover)
978-1-63235-105-0 (paperback)
978-1-62143-086-5 (hosted ebook)

Library of Congress Control Number: 2014937414

Printed in the United States of America
Mankato, MN
June, 2014

TABLE OF CONTENTS

CHAPTER 1

HIGH SCHOOL HERO

"Gooooooooaal!" Logan Parrish shouted at the top of his lungs.

On the soccer field in front of him, Logan's older brother, Elliot, had just kicked a slicing shot past the opponent's goalie and into the net. Elliot was captain of the East Grover Lake High School Grizzlies soccer team. He was a junior, and the team's starting center midfielder. He also led the team in goals.

This goal gave the Grizzlies a 1-0 lead.

Logan and his friends watched from the metal bleachers set up around the field. It was a chilly evening. Annie Roger had her brown, curly hair hidden beneath a floppy stocking cap. Next to her, Ben Mason wore a black puffy coat and a baseball cap pulled low. And Gabe Santiago was polishing off a giant mug filled with steaming hot chocolate. Now, they were all on their feet, chanting together at the top of their lungs. "Grizzlies! Grizzlies! Grrrrrr!"

"That was wild," Gabe said when the crowd quieted a bit.

"Yeah, he's pretty awesome." Logan smiled, but his heart fluttered with a twinge of jealousy at the comment. He knew Elliot worked hard at soccer, but his skills made Logan envious.

Probably because Mom and Dad worship the ground he walks on, Logan thought.

Logan looked down at the sidelines. His parents, both wearing the Grizzlies' colors, red and brown, stood as close to the action as they could get.

The four friends cheered as the action on the field resumed. A Grizzlies' forward shuffled past a midfielder for the opposing team and raced toward the corner. Before he reached it, however, he sent a pass into the middle of the field, right at Elliot.

Elliot broke toward the goal, dribbling the ball effortlessly between his feet. One of the opposing team's defenders ran up from the penalty arc to challenge him. Elliot faked left and sprung right. He planted his left foot and sent a sailing shot at the goal.

The goalie dove . . .

. . . and *just* missed tipping the ball away with his fingers.

The ball struck the back of the net.

The crowd roared.

"Two goals in one minute?! Wow!" Gabe was flabbergasted.

Each high school game was broken into two halves lasting forty minutes apiece. By the end of the first half, Elliot and the Grizzles had a two-goal lead, 3-1.

During halftime, Logan and his friends hit the concession stand for more hot chocolate and treats. As they stood in line, Gabe said,

"So, we've got tryouts for the EGL Middle School *futbol* team—"

"Football?" Ben interrupted. "It's not football season, man."

Gabe rolled his eyes. "*Futbol*," he said. "You know, the name everyone else in the world calls soccer?"

"I knew what you meant," Annie piped in.

"Thank you," Gabe continued. "Tryouts for the . . . s*occer* . . . team are this Monday. Anyone want to join me?"

Ben shook his head. "No thanks."

"Logan? What do you say?"

Gabe had been playing soccer for years, but Logan had never tried out for the team. He played a number of other sports. Baseball. Basketball. *American* football.

However, watching his brother out on the field made the idea of playing soccer really appealing. Elliot made it look easy, effortless. Maybe Logan could play like that, too.

"Yeah," Logan said. "I'll give it a shot."

"Cool!" Gabe offered him a fist bump, and Logan accepted.

The gang returned to their seats just as the ref blew his whistle to start the second half.

Elliot picked up right where he left off. He covered every inch of the field. What made him a good leader was his ability not just to score, but also to pass. When the right forward broke into the open, Elliot skirted the ball quickly along the grass. The forward booted it at the net, and the Grizzlies racked up another goal.

By the end of the game, the Grizzlies had won easily by a score of 5–2.

Elliot and his team shook hands with their opponents and then huddled together on the sidelines for a victory cheer.

As Logan joined Elliot and his parents on the sidelines for a celebratory hug and high five, he thought about tryouts and wondered if he could live up to the Parrish name on the soccer field.

CHAPTER 2

AN AMAZING FIND

All the members of the Parrish family— except Logan—were early risers. His father and brother jogged each morning before most of Grover Lake had even cracked open their eyes. Their mom preferred to enjoy a cup of coffee and the newspaper before work.

"Remember, the early bird gets the worm," his dad said like clockwork each morning.

"And the second mouse gets the cheese," his mom countered every time.

11

She had her own way of staying fit, though, one that included yoga and Pilates classes at the community center.

The morning after Elliot's game, a Saturday, Logan was awakened by the sound of his brother knocking on his door. Elliot wore a school T-shirt, black shorts, and running shoes.

"Morning, little bro," he said.

Logan sat up, wiped the sleep from his eyes, and grunted like a caveman.

"Dad and I are about to head out for a jog. Then I'm supposed to take you and Gabe over to Sal's before I go to work. Right?"

"Uh-huh." The last time Logan and Gabe had been at Sal's Used Sporting Goods, the store's owner, Sal Horton, recruited them to help him move some bulky equipment before the store opened for the weekend.

"Cool," Elliot said. "Back in a flash."

Logan dressed and went downstairs to wait. He sat on a stool at the kitchen counter and ate a bowl of cereal while his mom worked on a Sudoku puzzle.

When Elliot and Logan's dad returned from their run, Elliot showered and changed into his work clothes: khaki pants and a blue polo shirt with the name Speedy Subs—a sandwich shop in the mall—stitched onto it.

Logan rode shotgun in Elliot's sleek car. He'd gotten the ride from their parents on his sixteenth birthday. Elliot cranked up the stereo's volume, and the bass pumping from the speakers and subwoofers made the windows rattle.

Gabe was waiting for them on his front porch. He waved, jumped down the steps, and dashed across his lawn to the car.

Sal's was located in a brick building along a strip of small businesses in downtown Grover Lake. A faded orange awning shaded the plate-glass window bearing the store's name.

Elliot dropped them off at the curb. Even though the store wasn't technically open yet, its front door was unlocked.

Sal's was a cluttered mess, packed with shelves upon shelves of athletic equipment. It boggled Logan's mind to think that Sal knew where everything was located.

As they entered, Logan saw the shop's owner standing on a stool down the store's main aisle.

"There they are!" Sal lumbered down off the stool. He had a barrel chest, thinning hair, and a gray beard.

"Mornin', Sal," Logan said.

"*Hola*," Gabe added.

"Thank you boys so much for coming down this morning." Sal walked over to the glass counter located along the east wall of the store. The case held many signed and rare items. The wall behind the counter was covered in framed photos of athletes.

"Follow me," Sal said as he stepped behind the glass counter and motioned for them to join him. Logan felt strange, as if he was entering forbidden territory by stepping beyond the counter's threshold.

They passed through a door that led to a hallway and stairs heading to the store's basement. At the end of the hall was a loading dock. There, leaning against the wall, were six kayaks.

"A friend dropped them off the other day," Sal said, his voice echoing off the walls. "They aren't heavy, just cumbersome enough to be a two-person job."

"We got this," Logan said confidently. "Shouldn't take too long."

"Excellent." Sal lumbered back in the direction of the store.

As Logan and Gabe maneuvered the first kayak down the hall, Gabe asked, "So, you pumped for soccer tryouts on Monday?"

"Yeah, man," Logan said. "Of course."

"You're not gonna back out, are you?"

"What? No way."

"Cool. Coach Hessman's gonna be thrilled you're trying out."

"He is?" Logan's pulse quickened. He knew there'd be expectations surrounding him. After all, Coach Hessman had been Elliot's coach when he was in middle school. But it wasn't until Gabe mentioned it out loud that Logan's nerves kicked in. His hands grew clammy and cold, and he nearly lost his grip on the kayak.

One by one, they moved the colorful kayaks to the store, lining them against one wall. It took them less than a half hour to complete the job.

When they were finished, Sal came over and marveled at their work. "Wonderful!" he exclaimed, clapping his hands. "As a reward, I'd like to offer you both one item from the store. Yours for the taking, free of charge." He winked and added, "Within reason, of course."

"Awesome!" Gabe said eagerly. "Thanks, Sal!"

Gabe and Logan split up and wandered the aisles like kids in a candy shop. Logan looked at baseball mitts and bowling balls and even a paintball helmet.

But then he spied it.

A wire rack filled with soccer balls had been set up at the end of one aisle. A sign above the rack read: *$10 EACH*. Many were old and scuffed, or smaller than regulation size.

Perched perfectly atop the pile, though, was a new, traditional black and white ball.

Something drew Logan to it. He couldn't say what, but he was certain that he wanted this to be his payment.

As he scooped the ball off the top of the pile, he noticed something scribbled across the ball in silver marker. It was a name.

Logan's jaw nearly scraped the dusty floor.

It said: *David Beckham.*

CHAPTER 3

COULD IT REALLY BE?

Logan stared at the soccer ball, stunned.

No way. Something this valuable would be locked behind the glass counter, with all the other signed memorabilia.

Logan reached out, expecting a booby trap to snap up when he plucked the soccer ball from its spot. Nothing happened, though. No nets from above. No blow darts. No giant boulders squashing him like a bug.

Logan examined the autograph more closely. "It's gotta be a fake," he muttered.

Still, he'd been drawn like a magnet to this particular soccer ball for a reason. So he tucked it under his arm, hid the autograph beneath his cradled palm, and rejoined Sal and Gabe at the counter.

"Whatcha got?" Gabe inquired. He spun a football in nice condition around in the palm of his hand. "Check out this bad boy."

A lump had grown in Logan's throat as his nerves swelled. He swallowed it down. "Is it okay if I have this soccer ball, Sal?"

Sal's eyes narrowed.

He knows, Logan thought. *It's real, and I'm busted.*

But then Sal just nodded and said, "Perfectly all right. I'm sure it will come in handy, Logan. Thanks again, boys!"

"*Gracias*, Sal," Gabe said.

"Yeah. Thanks." Logan led the way quickly out of the store. Guilt was wrapping its claws around his chest.

A cool breeze and late-morning sunlight helped to break its spell. It was a perfect morning to walk home. Logan and Gabe strolled down the sidewalk, through Grover Lake's older section of town.

As they reached a residential area, where front lawns were lined up like squares on a quilt, Gabe suggested, "Hey, let's kick your new ball around a bit to practice for Monday's tryouts."

Logan shook his head. "No way, man."

Gabe jogged down the sidewalk in front of Logan. "Come on, fire it my way."

"I don't wanna practice right now, okay?" Logan had no intention of letting this ball touch the ground.

"Whatever." Gabe shrugged.

The two friends walked in silence until they reached Gabe's house. Logan lived about ten blocks from Gabe. He took a shortcut through yards until he made it home.

Logan hurried inside and took the steps to the second floor two at a time, ending at Elliot's closed bedroom door. It was a common brotherly rule that entering one another's rooms without consent was a crime punished with a charley horse. Today, Logan was willing to take that risk.

Elliot's room was a disaster zone. Clothes were piled everywhere. The walls were plastered with posters featuring his favorite athletes, including a few soccer players.

A poster of Barcelona's legendary Lionel Messi hung over Elliot's desk. Another next to it showcased Landon Donovan.

But the one Logan was looking for was taped to the wooden closet door. It showed David Beckham midgame with Manchester United, his right leg following through on a kick, and a soccer ball looming large, as if it was about to bust free of the poster.

In looping letters at the bottom, as part of the poster design, was Beckham's signature. Logan held his new soccer ball next to the poster.

The signatures looked nearly identical.

That doesn't mean anything. Anyone could have taken a Sharpie and written on it.

But something in his gut told him it was probably real.

Logan left Elliot's room without disturbing a thing. *Like Elliot could tell I was in there anyway*, he thought as he closed the door again. *I could have detonated a grenade and he wouldn't notice.*

He carried the ball back to his own room, where he examined it closely one more time. He needed to take it back to Sal.

I will, he promised himself. *Just . . . later.*

And then he squirreled the ball away under his bed, where no one would find it and no one would ask questions.

CHAPTER 4

LIKE BROTHER, LIKE BROTHER?

"All right, let's do this!"

Gabe, who was so excited he looked as if he'd drunk about a water tower's worth of energy drinks, slapped Logan on the back. The two friends—decked out in red and brown school T-shirts, shorts, and shin guards hidden by knee-high socks—walked out of the locker room at East Grover Lake Middle School and into the blinding afternoon sunlight.

Logan took a deep breath and exhaled slowly. For the most part, he was still pumped to try out for the team. But there was a part of him that was very nervous.

A number of boys were already scattered on the field. Logan recognized almost all of them. Some wore jerseys from last season—including the team captain and striker, the tall and angular Tyler Murphy—but there were some newcomers like Logan.

A man in his forties wearing a Grizzlies cap and a pair of wraparound sunglasses stood nearby. He was peering down at his clipboard.

"*Hola*, Coach Hessman," Gabe said.

Coach Hessman looked up. He smiled and said, "Santiago, good to see you. And if it isn't the one and only Logan Parrish."

He held out his hand. Logan, momentarily taken aback, didn't know what to do. Then he reached over and shook it.

"Great to have another Parrish prodigy in our ranks. If you're half as good as your brother, you'll be a fine asset to the team."

"Uh, thanks," Logan said. He noticed a couple of boys nearby, newcomers as well, listening in on their conversation.

Coach Hessman blew his whistle, and the boys huddled together around the field's center circle. "Welcome," he said. "Today, we're going to run through a few drills to see how well you dribble, pass, and shoot. Many of you played together last year, but that doesn't automatically earn you a spot this time around. We've got a few new faces that are sure to surprise us."

Logan couldn't be certain, but he was pretty sure Coach Hessman was talking about him.

They split into groups of three. Logan was teamed with Gabe and Scotty, another boy who'd played on the team before.

"This is a passing drill," Coach Hessman explained. "A three-man weave. When you get close to the goal, take a shot." He blew his whistle, and the first team navigated down the field. After each pass, the person who sent the ball forward ran over and slid behind the player who received the pass. Logan was familiar with the drill; he had executed it many times on the basketball court.

When it was their turn, Gabe quickly dribbled the ball up the field. He passed over to Scotty, who took it midstride and booted it over to Logan. Logan bobbled it with his left foot. The ball skittered forward. Logan raced after it.

"Keep your head up!" Coach Hessman shouted. "Watch where you're going and anticipate the pass!"

Frustrated and embarrassed, Logan sent the ball flying toward Gabe. Then he ran over and behind his friend, cursing under his breath.

By the time they'd reached the rectangular penalty area, Logan had the ball. He hastily took a shot at the unguarded goal. It sailed wide, missing by a good five feet.

"Pfft! Nice shot," Scotty grumbled.

"That's all right!" Coach Hessman shouted. "Hustle up! You'll get it next time."

But the next time down, Logan didn't take a shot. He sent the ball to Gabe, who easily scored on the open net.

For the next two hours, the boys worked on a variety of passing and shooting drills. Logan felt overwhelmed. There was so much he didn't know about soccer. How to get a shot off using power and accuracy. How to use his head and chest to pass and receive the ball. How to stop the ball by trapping it with one cleat.

He was out of his league.

The only person on the field who thought he was doing all right was Coach Hessman. Logan could sense everyone else snickering at him or saying things about him behind his back.

Coach Hessman blew his whistle and shouted, "Bring it in!" When the boys had surrounded him once more, he said, "Great work today. You boys have fire and determination, and you all deserve a spot on the team. I'll have to make some hard choices, but the final roster will be posted on the locker room door at the end of school Thursday."

The team dispersed, heading back to the locker room. Logan stopped at the sidelines and wiped down his sweaty face with his T-shirt. Coach Hessman walked past, turning and saying, "Nice work out there, Parrish."

Logan wished he could believe him.

CHAPTER 5

THE ROSTER

"Come on, come on," Gabe whispered from behind Logan.

It was Thursday, and Coach Hessman would be posting the soccer team roster after school. Logan and Gabe were sitting in their last class of the day, geography, and Gabe was watching the hands on the clock hanging above the whiteboard, almost willing time to speed up.

"Stop breathing on my neck," Logan hissed. He chucked a pencil over his shoulder at Gabe's desk. "You ate sloppy joes for lunch, dude, and your breath reeks."

"Sorry. I'm just . . . *excited*."

"Really? It's hard to tell." Sarcasm dripped off Logan's words.

Finally, after what felt like eons of listening to Gabe count off each minute, the buzzer sounded.

"About time," Gabe said, shuffling his books into a stack and picking them up. He made a beeline for the door.

"Dude, wait up." Logan hurried to catch up with his friend. Though he really wanted to be on the team, Logan didn't want to get his hopes up. He'd replayed the lowlights from tryouts in his head time and time again, like watching a horror movie on repeat.

The halls were filled with bustling kids. Most were digging their backpacks and books from their lockers. Others loitered in the middle of the hall, blocking traffic, just so they could talk.

Gabe was already halfway down the hall. Logan dodged Timmy Corbin, who was lugging his enormous tuba case toward the band room. He narrowly avoided a gaggle of girls sharing photos on their phones and nearly took out a teacher carrying an armload of textbooks.

"Slow in the halls," the teacher's thunderous voice commanded.

"Sorry," Logan said. He slowed to a fast walk until the teacher was out of sight and then broke back into a run.

About a dozen boys were crowding around the door to the locker room. As Logan approached, Gabe spun on a heel, pumped a fist, and said, "Oh yeah. Never a doubt."

"You made the team?" Logan asked.

"Yep."

"Did I?" Logan peered over shoulders at the locker room door, where a single sheet of white paper had been stuck up with athletic tape. A list of names typed in all capital letters ran down the page. About thirty kids had tried out, and Coach Hessman had whittled that down to twenty-two.

About halfway down the alphabetized list was the name *LOGAN PARRISH*.

Wow. I did it! I'm on the team!

Logan tried to act cool, as if making the squad was no biggie.

Around him, Logan noticed a few other boys upset at not making the team. Suddenly, he was wracked with guilt. He couldn't help but think that Coach Hessman had given him special treatment and that he'd only made the team because of his last name and his brother's history with the team.

His good mood spoiled, Logan lowered his head and hurried back through the hall, as far away from the locker room as he could get.

CHAPTER **6**

SCRIMMAGE

"Okay, everyone! Hustle it up!"

Coach Hessman sharply blew his whistle. Logan and his teammates, who had been running drills, jogged over to the sidelines. Logan was sweaty, his chest heaving. Sure, he was athletic, but soccer players were constantly in motion. It didn't help that Logan always felt a few steps behind the other players.

He lifted the neck of his red and brown jersey and used it to wipe the sweat from his forehead and nose.

Coach Hessman reached into a duffel bag slung over his shoulder and began to toss out two different-colored mesh jerseys. One was red, the other brown. "Time for a little friendly scrimmage," he explained as Logan snatched a red jersey out of the air. He looked over and saw Gabe pulling a brown jersey over his head.

When the teams were separated, the coach assigned positions. Tyler Murphy was the center midfielder for the red team. "Parrish, you're left forward," Coach Hessman barked. "Red team takes the first kickoff."

Logan jogged over to his position. Both teams set up in a 4-3-3 formation. That meant four defenders, three midfielders, and three forwards.

Tweet!

Coach Hessman dropped the ball in the center circle, and the game began.

Ty scanned the defense, then pushed the ball to the right forward, Scotty. Logan dashed down the field as Scotty weaved past two defenders. Scotty kept his eyes up, scanning the field. Logan had a clear shot at the goal. He stopped and waved an arm.

Scotty launched the ball off the side of his foot. Because Logan had stopped, though, the kick sailed wide. Logan instinctively reached out with both hands and slapped it out of the sky before it went out of bounds.

Tweet!

Coach Hessman shook his head. "Free kick from the spot of the foul for the brown team."

"What are you doing using your hands?" one of Logan's teammates, a kid named Max, asked.

"Sorry," Logan mumbled. "It was instinct."

Max shook his head, disappointed.

The brown team was awarded a free kick. After a bit of fancy footwork, their striker scored against the red team's goalie.

The next time down the field, the red team's offense deliberately kept the ball away from Logan. Ty even looked over at one point, saw Logan wide open, and instead rushed forward into two defenders.

Finally, after not touching the ball for most of the scrimmage, Logan decided he'd had enough. Scotty brought the ball up the right side of the field. Logan cut for the middle. When Scotty passed the ball toward Ty, Logan wanted to be there to intercept it.

He nearly made it. At the last second, Ty leaned forward, ready to use his head to advance the ball. Logan slammed into him hard, and they both fell to the grass, dazed and gasping for breath.

Coach Hessman and the rest of the team quickly rushed over to crowd around them.

Ty placed one hand on his head and said, "What are you doing, man? You could have hurt me."

Logan sat up and rubbed his arm, which throbbed with pain. "Just going after the ball."

"Well, you missed." Angry, Ty stood and stretched his lanky form.

"All right," Coach Hessman said with a clap, "let's call it a day. Remember, our first game against Prairie Hills is this Friday!"

The team broke and began to head back toward the school.

Logan and Gabe walked silently back to the locker room. They weaved through rows of blue metal lockers until they reached their lockers in the far corner.

As Logan changed into street clothes, he overheard a couple of his teammates speaking from the next row over.

"Man, whoever told me Parrish was as good as his brother was full of it," one said. Logan couldn't be sure, but it sounded like Scotty.

The second voice was clearly Tyler's. "Yeah, there's no reason he should be playing. Not when good players got cut from the team. He could have split my head open like a watermelon out there."

Logan, whose temper had a tendency to flare up at the worst of times, felt his cheeks flush and his hands shake. He slammed his locker door closed.

"Hey," Gabe said softly, "don't listen to them, man. They don't know what they're talking about."

Logan did not answer. He shouldered his bag and began to leave.

"Logan! Come on, man!" Gabe's voice echoed off the locker room walls. But Logan did not respond.

He exited the locker room, the door loudly banging closed behind him.

BROTHERLY WISDOM

Logan just wanted to be left alone. He wished that his bedroom were an island in the middle of nowhere, with no chance of a ship passing by or a plane circling overhead and certainly with no cell phone reception.

Gabe had tried to call him a few times that evening, but Logan kept hitting the red *IGNORE* button on his screen. Then Annie and Ben tried calling, too. Finally, Logan had turned his phone off and shoved it under his pillow.

At one point, his mom had knocked on his door and poked her head in. "Dinner in five minutes."

"I'm not hungry."

"All right, then." She'd gone, but a few minutes later, she returned with a plate of food and placed it on his desk. "Just in case you feel peckish," she said.

Logan dug under his bed, found the soccer ball from Sal's, and plucked it from its hiding place. He rolled it around in his hands, flipped it into the air, and ran his finger over the signature.

I bet David Beckham was never humiliated in front of his whole team.

Then, realizing he didn't actually know much about the soccer icon, Logan snatched his laptop off his desk and did an online search.

He read a brief bio of Beckham. As he did, he pulled the dinner plate onto his lap and ate the chicken, broccoli, and bread that his mother had brought him.

There was another knock on the door. This time, though, the newcomer burst in without waiting for Logan to tell him to get lost.

It was Elliot.

"Hey, little brother." Elliot wore his Speedy Subs shirt, and he smelled like meatballs and onions and fresh bread.

Logan, surprised, quickly stashed the soccer ball behind his back, under a blanket, nearly spilling his plate of food.

Elliot sat on the edge of the bed. "Mom told me you were up here moping. She thought it had something to do with soccer practice."

"It's nothing," Logan said.

"Really?"

Logan shrugged. "I made a fool out of myself during our scrimmage, and I'm pretty sure the team hates my guts. Except Gabe. He's my best friend, so he's legally obligated to have my back. He took an oath."

"That's nothing," Elliot said, waving a hand dismissively. "When I first started, I accidentally kicked the ball into my own goal. *Twice*. And I was the goalie."

Logan chuckled. Leave it to Elliot to make him feel a little better.

Elliot nodded at the laptop, which was still open to David Beckham's bio. A photo of the soccer pro filled most of the screen. "What are you reading?" he asked. "Doing a paper on him or something?"

"Or something." Logan didn't want to spill the real reason. He thought about the soccer ball under his blanket, and his insane guilt cranked itself up by a couple of notches.

"You know, Beckham used to be one of the smallest guys on the field," Elliot said.

"Really?"

"Yep. He had to work extra hard to be the best. Nothing that's worth doing comes easy, Logan." Elliot stood, stretched his back, and added, "Tell you what. Grab your cleats and meet me downstairs in five. 'Kay?"

"For what?"

Elliot smirked. "It's a surprise."

It was after dark, close to Logan's curfew, but because he was with Elliot, his parents let it slide. "Just don't be late," their dad said.

"Cross our hearts and hope to croak," Elliot replied.

Logan climbed into the passenger seat of Elliot's car and crammed the backpack containing his cleats onto the floor in front of him. "So, you going to tell me where we're going?"

Elliot shook his head, backed out of the driveway, and took off down the road. "Patience, bro," he said, cranking up the stereo's volume.

They wove through Grover Lake, lit now by streetlamps, past the high school and the mall. On the outskirts of town, Elliot took a left, onto a narrow blacktop road.

Logan was beyond confused. There was nothing out here but trees and farmland. Why would Elliot be taking him to the middle of nowhere?

When they reached a gravel road nearly hidden by trees, Elliot turned right. He flicked on his brights, cautiously rumbling down the dirt road.

Up on his left, Logan made out a faint glow emanating from the trees. "What is that?" he asked, pointing.

Elliot laughed. "Aliens."

They broke past the tree line and into a clearing. Logan could finally see the source of the glow. Two rows of cars faced one another, about fifty yards apart. Their headlights lit up the grassy clearing between them. Boys and girls, all high school age, gathered in the middle. Some kicked around soccer balls.

Goals had been set up on both sides of the makeshift field.

"Whoa," Logan said under his breath.

Elliot smiled. "Welcome to our weekly pickup game."

CHAPTER 8

NIGHT MOVES

Elliot parked at the end of one row of cars.
He shut the engine off, but left the headlights on, like all the others. "Are you ready?" he asked.

Logan shook his head. "No way I'm playing with a bunch of high schoolers," he said. "They're going to run circles around me."

"You'll be fine," Elliot said. "We're just playing for fun. Besides, your ol' pal Beckham gained experience playing against older kids and his dad's friends all the time."

"Really?" Logan looked out the windshield at the tall, imposing teenagers gathered on the field. One bounced a ball off his knee as if it was no big deal.

"Come on," Elliot said, cracking open his door. "Let's go have some fun."

Logan tentatively followed his brother, slinging his backpack over one shoulder. He recognized a few of Elliot's friends, guys from the varsity soccer team.

"Elliot, is this your little brother?" one of the girls asked.

"Yeah, this is Logan."

"Cool. Hey, Logan."

"Um . . . hi."

A number of kids nearby offered their hellos. Logan waved back at them.

He and Elliot changed into their cleats as one of the boys, a midfielder named Jesse Russell, split the group into two teams. Logan and Elliot wound up on the same team. "You wanna play forward?" Elliot asked as they walked to the center of the field.

"Uh, yeah. Sure." Logan's hands were shaking, and his heart was thudding in his chest. He lined up to the left of his brother, squinting in the strange headlight glare.

"Here we go!" Jesse shouted. He stood opposite Elliot. They slapped high five. Then Jesse dropped the ball between them.

Immediately, Elliot kicked the ball to his left, toward Logan. Logan panicked, but stopped the ball with his foot and began to dribble forward. He weaved his way down the field, running faster than ever.

A defender rushed up to meet him and easily snatched the ball away.

The opposing team passed the ball up to their forwards.

"Get it back!" Elliot shouted from midfield.

Jesse got the ball, and as a defender slid across the grass toward him, he booted it right at the goalie.

The goalie trapped and held the ball.

"Nice save, Dylan!" Elliot yelled through cupped hands.

For a time, both teams fought over the ball down on the far side of the field, but finally, it soared past midfield. Elliot swiftly took the ball and pushed it off the inside of his foot, right at Logan.

Again, Logan dribbled toward the goal.

Again, a defender stole it from him.

"Hold up!" Elliot shouted. Play stopped. "Give me the ball a sec." The girl with the ball kicked it over to him.

Logan was embarrassed. Everyone was staring at him.

What is Elliot doing?

Elliot placed the ball between them. "Let me show you something," he said. "It's called a step-over. You make it look like you are going to touch the ball to one side. But instead, you step over the ball, then push it to the other side with the outside of your foot." Elliot demonstrated the move slowly.

"Like that. See? The defender will bite, and you'll have a great breakaway."

"Cool. Um, thanks," Logan said quietly.

"Oh, and one other thing."

"What's that?"

Elliot punched him on the shoulder and said, "Loosen up, bro. Have some fun." He chucked the ball back to the opposing team member. "Game on!"

The other team scooted the ball upfield. An outside midfielder kicked it straight up in front of her and then used her head to bounce it over the defender to a waiting Jesse Russell. Jesse then skied a soaring shot that curved right past the goalie.

It was one of the coolest assists Logan had ever seen.

They played for a couple of hours, taking occasional breaks to drink water and joke around. After a shaky start, Logan calmed down and actually started to enjoy himself. They didn't keep score, but that didn't matter.

Near the end of the game, after one of Logan's teammates blocked a pass, the ball skittered his way. Logan made a break for the goal. He had one defender to beat. He thought about Elliot's advice and decided to go for it.

He stepped over the ball and pushed the other way awkwardly. Still, the defender went right, realized Logan was moving left, and fell while trying to correct his error.

It worked!

Logan had a free shot at the goal. He lined it up, reared back, and kicked.

Ping!

The shot struck the top of the goal's metal frame and sailed wide.

Elliot jogged up and slapped him on the back. "That's what I'm talking 'bout, bro!"

It was getting late by the time they all went their separate ways. The players all shook hands, and many of them asked Logan if he was going to join them again next week.

"Maybe," he replied with a smile. "It *is* past my bedtime, though."

They all got a good laugh out of his comment.

Together, Logan and Elliot walked back to their car. As they climbed in, Logan said, "Hey Elliot. Thanks for bringing me."

"No prob, little brother," Elliot said. "No prob at all."

CHAPTER 9

GAME TIME!

The first game of the Grizzlies' season was at home, against a team from a nearby town, the Prairie Hills Eagles. Logan's parents and friends sat together in the front row of the bleachers. Elliot, who had to work after the game, wore his Speedy Subs shirt.

"Grizzlies! Grizzlies! Grrrrrr!" Annie and Ben chanted with the crowd as Logan, Gabe, and their teammates took the field. Logan was still mad at Scotty and Tyler, but he was more determined than ever to prove he deserved to be on the team.

Gabe, who was very superstitious, never washed his jersey. The wrinkled, smelly old thing hadn't been cleaned since last season. He took the field with the rest of the starters. Logan stayed on the sidelines, ready to sub in.

"All right, guys! Stay alert out there!" Coach Hessman clapped loudly as the Grizzlies won the coin toss and Tyler Murphy prepared for the kickoff.

Ty kicked the ball right to Gabe, a forward. Gabe was quick and easily weaved past one defender. He bounced the ball back to Ty, who took the pass off his chest and dribbled downfield. An Eagle defender slid at him, booting the ball away. A second defender sent it sailing out past midfield.

The teams were evenly matched, moving the ball from one end of the field to the other. Once, the striker for the Eagles had a clear shot, but the Grizzlies' goalie, Gus, dove in front of it, and the ball ricocheted off his chest.

"Nice save!" Logan shouted. He had determined that his feelings about his teammates could wait; he cared more about winning.

The next time down the field, a Grizzlies winger headed the ball over a defender. Gabe gobbled up the pass and sent a powerful kick toward the upper section of the goal.

Nothing but net.

"Goal!" shouted the ref.

Gabe pumped a fist. As he ran past the sideline, Logan reached out, and the two friends slapped five.

Later in the half, Coach Hessman finally barked out, "Subs!" Logan dashed out onto the field, taking his position at left forward.

The Eagles took the kickoff into Grizzlies territory, but the defense was playing well, and Scotty intercepted a pass and sent the ball soaring high in the air. Ty tracked it down, leaped high, and headed it toward Logan.

Logan dribbled downfield. He kept his head up as much as he could. Ty was open in the middle, and he sent the ball skittering toward him.

Ty planted his leg and kicked a monster shot that clanged off the metal side post, struck the stunned goalie's shoulder, and went in.

Tweet!

"Goal!"

As Logan jogged to the sidelines, Ty ran over and offered his fist. "Nice assist, Parrish," he said.

Logan took this as an apology for the things he overheard Ty saying in the locker room. He decided to forgive and forget, and bumped Ty's fist with his own. "Great shot, man," he said.

The score remained the same for the rest of the first half and into the second, before the Eagles' striker found the back of the net to make the score 2-1. An illegal tackle led to a Grizzlies penalty, and on the ensuing penalty kick, the Grizzlies tied it up.

Logan played more minutes than he expected. He was winded, exhausted. But his adrenaline pushed him forward.

With only a minute left, and the game tied, the Grizzles gained control of the ball. One of the midfielders brought it across the halfway line and was immediately swarmed by defenders.

"Over here!"

Logan was wide open. Finding a gap in the defense, the midfielder passed it up to him.

Time was running out. Logan broke for the goal. There was one defender left to beat. He thought back to the night game, to Elliot's instructions on how to use a step-over to fake out a defender.

As he crossed into the penalty area, Logan moved his left foot over the ball, and the defender lunged in that direction, just as Logan hoped. Then he dribbled left, and the defender, unable to recover quickly, slid back at the ball, but kicked Logan instead. They both tumbled to the grass.

The ref blew his whistle. "Penalty kick, Grizzlies!" he shouted.

There were only a few seconds left on the clock. All the players looked to the Grizzlies' bench to see who Coach Hessman would choose to take the kick. "Parrish!" the coach barked. "You take it. You earned it!"

Logan lined up for the penalty kick of his life. It would also be his first shot on goal in the entire game.

"Come on, Logan!" he heard Annie shout from the crowd.

"You can do it!" Gabe added from the sidelines.

Logan took a deep breath. "Loosen up," he muttered to himself. "Have fun."

Without taking his eyes off the goalie, Logan ran up for the kick. He planted his foot, positioned his chest and chin over the ball, and struck the middle of the ball with the inside of his foot.

The shot sailed high and to the goalie's left. The keeper dove, but there was no way he was going to stop Logan's shot. It rocketed past him like a blur. The ball caught the net perfectly.

"Goal!" the ref shouted.

With little time left on the clock, the Eagles were unable to mount an attack.

Logan leaped into the air. He'd scored the game-winning goal. The Grizzlies surrounded him, slapping him on the back and congratulating one another.

When the celebration had dispersed a bit, Logan broke free and jogged to the sideline, where his parents and brother waited.

"What a wonderful game, Logan," his mom said. "So exciting."

"We're very proud of you," his dad added.

Elliot punched him on the shoulder. "Great step-over, bro," he said. "Where'd you learn that?" Then, laughing, he picked Logan up in a crushing bear hug.

CHAPTER 10

RETURN

There was one thing Logan needed to do, and he'd put off doing it long enough.

The morning after his first game, Logan stuffed the David Beckham-signed soccer ball into his backpack, hopped on his bike, and rode through town to Sal's.

As Logan walked through the front door, his nerves kicked in. The store was empty except for Sal, who sat behind the counter, a crossword puzzle in front of him, chewing on the eraser end of a pencil. Quiet music filtered from an antique radio behind him on a shelf.

Sal looked up as the bell above the door jingled. "Ah, good morning, Logan," he said.

"Morning, Sal." Logan was surprised that his dry mouth could form words.

"What brings you in this fine day?"

"Well," Logan fumbled with his backpack, unzipping it with one hand and scooping out the soccer ball with the other. "I wanted to bring this back to you."

Sal's face scrunched up as he considered the ball. "Ah, yes," he said. "Your payment for helping me last week. Why would you want to return it?"

Logan showed Sal the autograph. "This." He pointed to Beckham's name. Then he walked over and set the ball on the counter in front of Sal. "Is it real?"

Sal smiled and picked up the ball. "Indeed it is. Signed on one of my trips out to Los Angeles, at a Galaxy soccer match."

"So you knew the autograph was real when you gave it to me?"

Sal nodded. "I figured it was in good hands. Also, that you would return it when the time was right."

"What do you mean?"

"Just that sometimes, we need a helping hand or two when getting the feel of a new sport," Sal said cryptically. Then he slid open the glass case, made room between a Joe Montana-signed football and a Lou Gehrig baseball card, and placed the soccer ball on the shelf. He faced the autograph out for customers to see.

"You know, the soccer balls are still on display," Sal said as he locked the case. "You're more than welcome to take a replacement with you."

Logan smiled. "Thanks, Sal." He found the display, searched its contents until he found one he liked—a red and black regulation-size ball—and dug it out. Just to be sure, Logan quickly scanned the surface of the ball.

No autograph.

He said good-bye to Sal, thanked the shopkeeper once more, gave a last long look at the David Beckham ball, and exited the store.

Logan met his friends at Grover Park that afternoon. The sprawling park was filled with parents and children. Some played basketball on the single court, others tossed a Frisbee around, and still more climbed on the park's enormous playground.

"There he is," Ben said, "the dude with the game-winning kick!"

"Hey, we wouldn't have won if it weren't for my lucky jersey," Gabe said.

Logan jokingly plugged his nose. "That's because the other team couldn't breathe," he said in a nasal voice.

Gabe shrugged. "Whatever works, *amigo*."

Logan dropped his new soccer ball to the ground. Annie immediately ran up and snatched it away from him. "What are you slowpokes waiting for?" she asked as she broke from the trio of boys and out into the park's expansive, grassy field. "Catch me if you can!"

Logan laughed. Then he, Ben, and Gabe raced after her, content to spend their afternoon playing soccer together under a cloudless sky.

THE END

ABOUT THE AUTHOR

Brandon Terrell is a Saint Paul-based writer. He is the author of numerous children's books, including picture books, chapter books, and graphic novels. When not hunched over his laptop, Brandon enjoys watching movies and television, reading, baseball, and spending every spare moment with his wife and their two children.

ABOUT THE SOCCER STARS

Lionel Messi overcame a medical issue that affected his growth to become one of the world's best players.

Professional Team: FC Barcelona (Spain)

National Team: Argentina

Position: Striker

World Cup Appearances: 3, as of 2014

FIFA Player of the Year: 2009, 2010, 2011, 2012

Landon Donovan is the US National Team's all-time leader in both goals and assists.

Professional Team: Los Angeles Galaxy

National Team: USA

Position: Forward

World Cup Appearances: 3

US Soccer Athlete of the Year: 2003, 2004, 2009, 2010

David Beckham gained fame as one of the world's best players while with Manchester United FC (England), and then he helped popularize the sport in the United States by playing for Los Angeles Galaxy from 2007 to 2012.

Professional Team: Retired, last played for Paris Saint-Germain FC (France)

National Team: Retired, last played for England

Position: Midfielder

World Cup Appearances: 3

UEFA Best Midfielder: 1999

THINK ABOUT IT

1. At one point in the story, Elliot takes Logan to play with his friends. How would the story be different if this event hadn't happened? Would Logan still have succeeded at soccer?

2. When Logan picked the soccer ball with David Beckham's autograph in Sal's Used Sporting Goods store, do you feel it was wrong or right to take it as his reward for helping Sal? What would you do if you were Logan?

3. Read another Game On! story. In *Break for the Goal,* Logan succeeds with the help of his older brother. How is this different or similar to the other story you've read?

1. Near the beginning of the story, Logan and his friends call out "Grizzlies! Grizzlies! Grrrrrr!" after a goal is scored. Fans often yell and chant to support their team. Write a chant to shout out when your school team is playing.

2. Do you have a sibling, whether a brother or sister, older or younger? Logan looks up to his brother Elliot because he's a great soccer player. Write about the things you like about one of your siblings. Do you look up to him or her, or do you help them out like Elliot helped Logan?

3. What is your favorite sport? Why? Write down what you like about the sport, and compare it with other sports. What makes you like one sport more than another?

GET YOUR GAME ON!

Read more about Logan and his friends as they get their game on.

Blur on the Base Paths
Ben Mason needs to speed things up on the base paths, so he visits Sal's Used Sporting Goods to buy some different cleats and learns all about the Man of Steal, Rickey Henderson. Can Ben's vintage cleats help his team get past a showdown with their crosstown rivals?

Dive for the Goal Line
Gabe Santiago is a backup running back. On the day that he loses his lucky football gloves, the team's starting running back, Ben Mason, gets hurt. Now Gabe needs to get his game on as he is thrust into the starting running back role.

Drive to the Hoop
Annie Roger will do anything to prove that girls can play basketball just as good as boys. She heads over to Sal's Used Sporting Goods and learns all about Nancy Lieberman, a women's basketball legend. Can her newfound inspiration carry Annie and her friends to the championship?

READ MORE FROM 12-STORY LIBRARY

Every 12-Story Library book is available in many formats, including Amazon Kindle and Apple iBooks. For more information, visit your device's store or 12StoryLibrary.com.